For Richard and Tim S.N.

This edition published in 2001 by Zero to Ten Limited
327 High Street, Slough, Berkshire, SL1 1TX

Publisher: Anna McQuinn
Art Director: Tim Foster
Senior Editor: Simona Sideri
Publishing Assistant: Vikram Parashar

A CIP catalogue record for this book is available from the British Library.

ISBN: 1-84089-200-5

Printed in Hong Kong

MORE!

Illustrated by Sheilagh Noble

Look!

Walk!

Chatter

Chatter

Duck!

Quack!

Quack!

Up!

Dog!

Down!

Nice dog!

Swings!

Come on!

Push me!

Come on!

Where's Teddy?

Bye! Bye!

More Toddler Books from Zero to Ten

Whoops!

Yuck! Ouch! Mine! Bye Bye!
Two lively toddlers spend the day playing and
inevitably end up squabbling.

Hb with card pages ISBN: 1-84089-079-7
Pb with card page ISBN: 1-84089-125-4

Uh-oh!

Don't worry. Look! Share! Squishy! Your friend!
This title follows our little girl's first day at nursery school,
from the tentative first moments through her growing confidence
until Dad picks her up at the end of the day.

Hb with card pages ISBN: 1-84089-182-3

More books for young children from Zero to Ten

Things I Eat!

photographs by Hannah Tofts

"...The sumptuous fruits here really
do look good enough to eat..."
Junior Magazine

"...really caught our eye.
Their stunning photographic
images make them great
first word books..."
Practical Parenting

I Eat Fruit!
Hb ISBN 1-84089-117-3
Pb ISBN 1-84089-162-9

I Eat Vegetables!
Hb ISBN 1-84089-118-1
Pb ISBN 1-84089-163-7

Animal Worlds

illustrated by Paul Hess

'...delicious books'...
The Good Book Guide

"... first word books with a difference...
Each animal is exquisitely illustrated
and named in big, bold type."
Parents Magazine

Farmyard Animals Board Book
ISBN 1-84089-164-5

Safari Animals Board Book
ISBN 1-84089-165-3

Rainforest Animals Board Book
ISBN 1-84089-166-1

Polar Animals Board Book
ISBN 1-84089-167-X

Zero to Ten books are available from all good bookstores.
If you have any problems obtaining any title, or to order a catalogue, please contact the publishers:
Zero to Ten Ltd., 327 High Street, Slough, Berkshire SL1 1TX   Tel: 01753 578 499   Fax: 01753 578 488